Ballad of the Ice Fairy

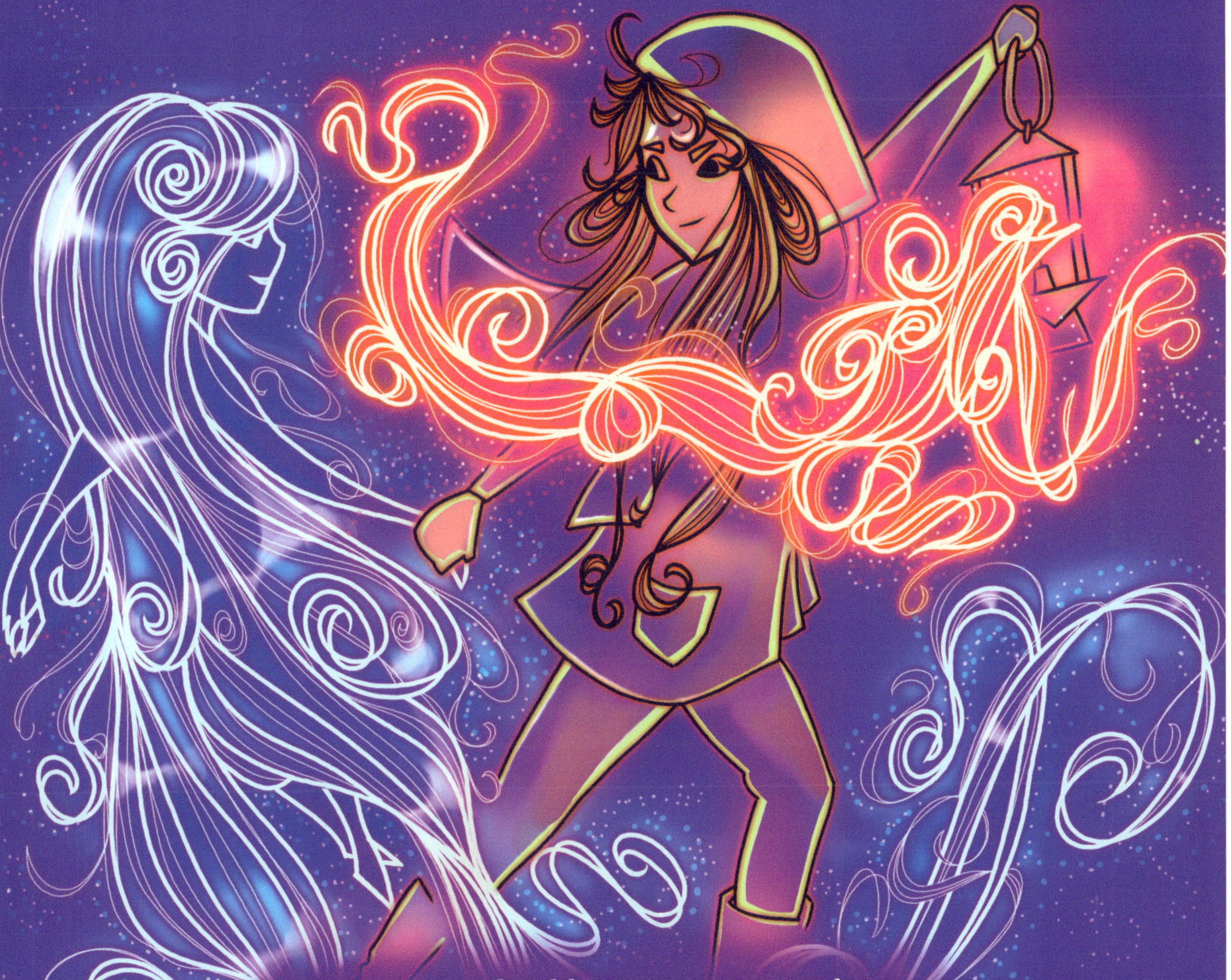

Story and Illustrations by
award-winning fantasy author

ELLIE RAINE

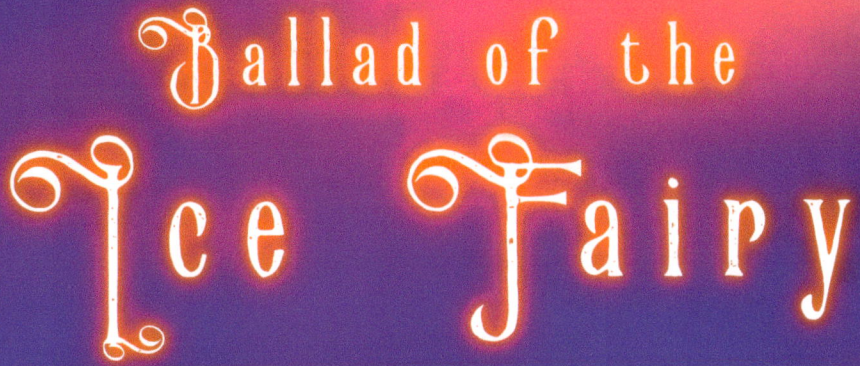

Ballad of the Ice Fairy
Text copyright © 2020 by Ellie Raine
Illustration copyright © 2020 by Ellie Raine

All rights reserved. This book or any portion thereof may not be reproduced or used in any manner whatsoever without the express written permission of the publisher except for the use of brief quotations in a book review or article.

This is a work of fiction. Concepts, Names, characters, businesses, places, events, locales, and incidents are either the products of the author's imagination or used in a fictitious manner. Any resemblance to actual persons, living or dead, or actual events is purely coincidental.

Printed in the United States of America
ISBNs: 978-1-953031-00-6
First Printing, Edition I: 2020
Published by
ScyntheFy Press, LLC
www.ScyntheFy.com

For information about special discounts available for bulk purchases, sales promotions, fund-raising and educational needs, contact ScyntheFy Press at: www.scynthefy.com/contact

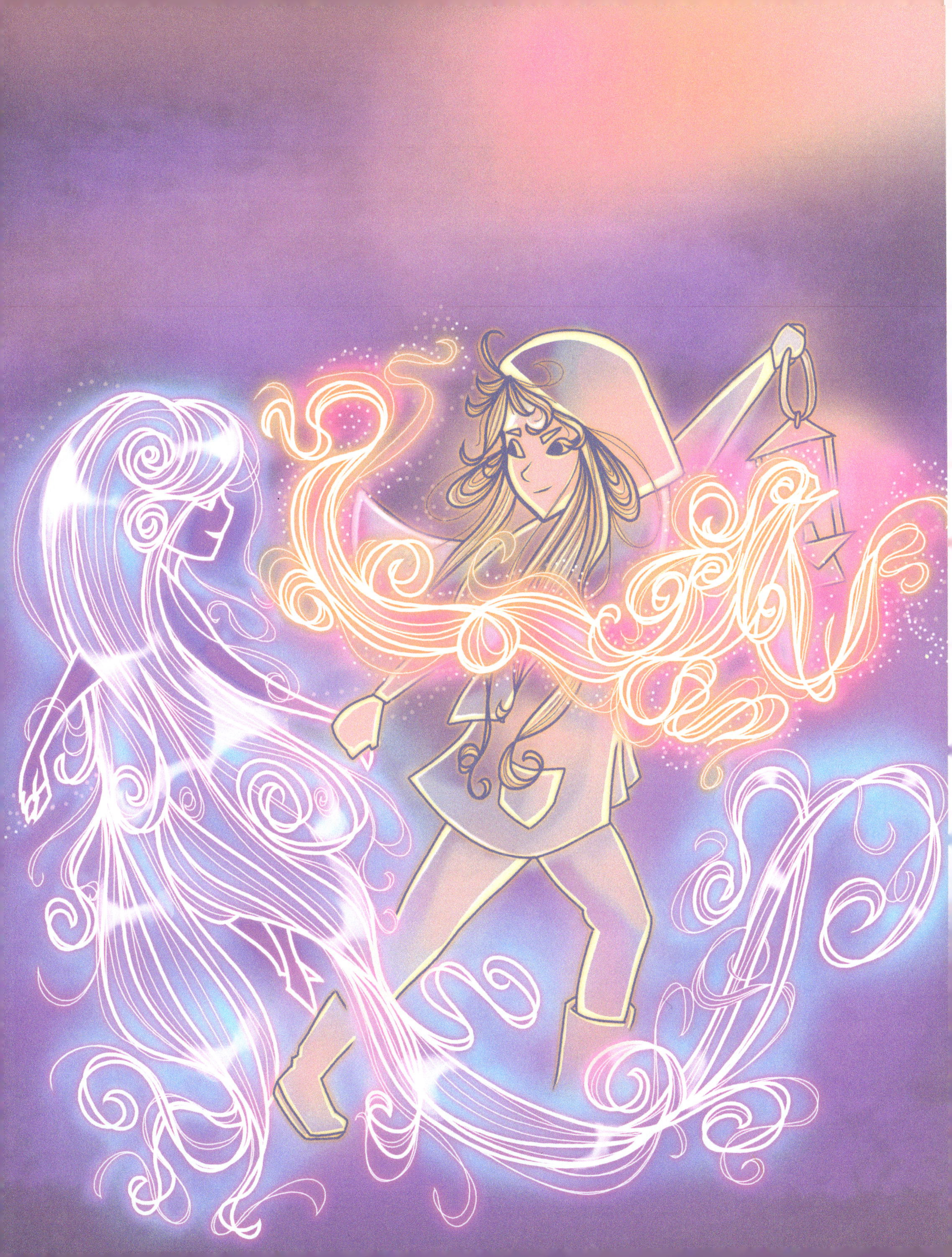

Dedication:

To those who have lost,
who keep their memories as guiding lights
that still warm the fire in their hearts.

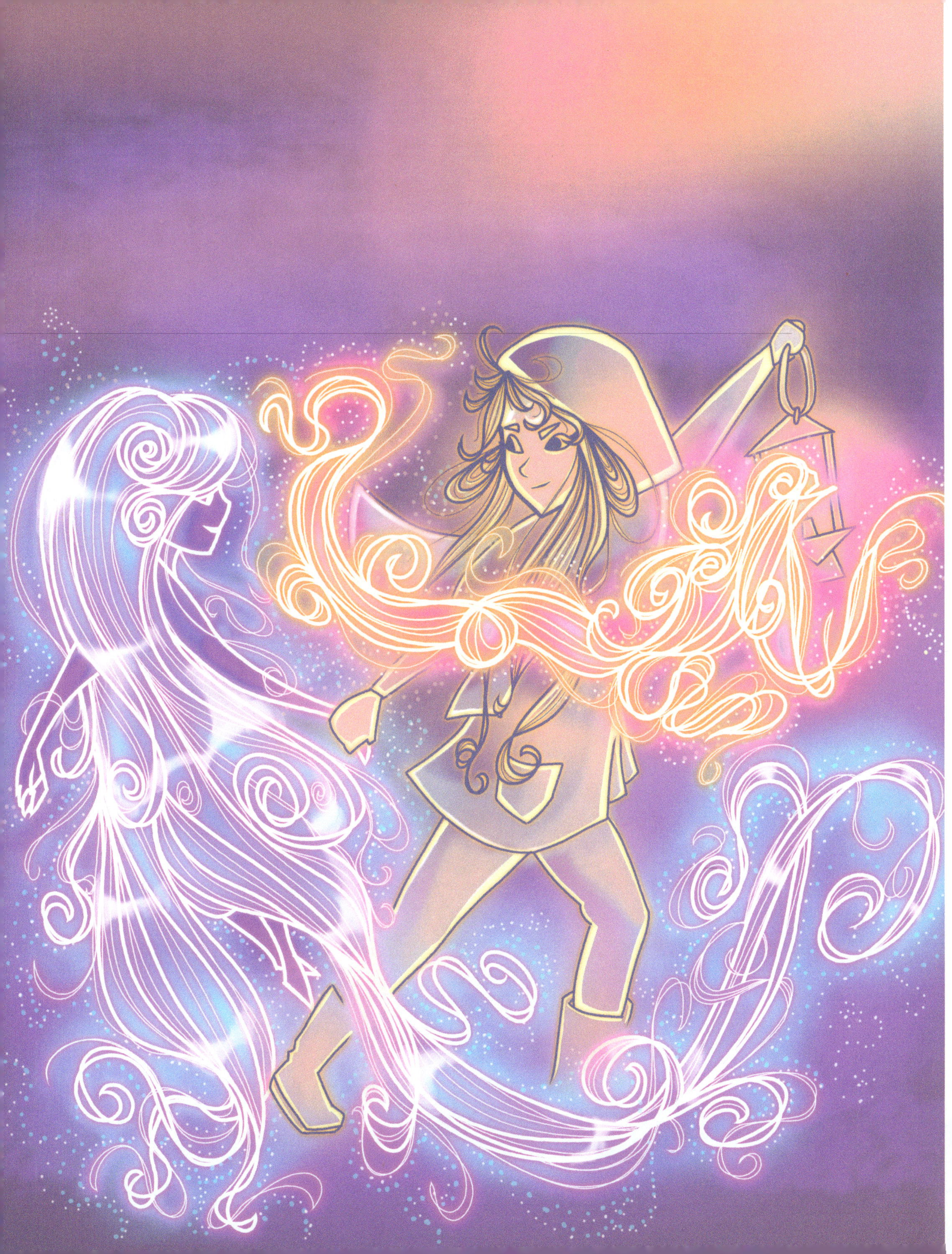

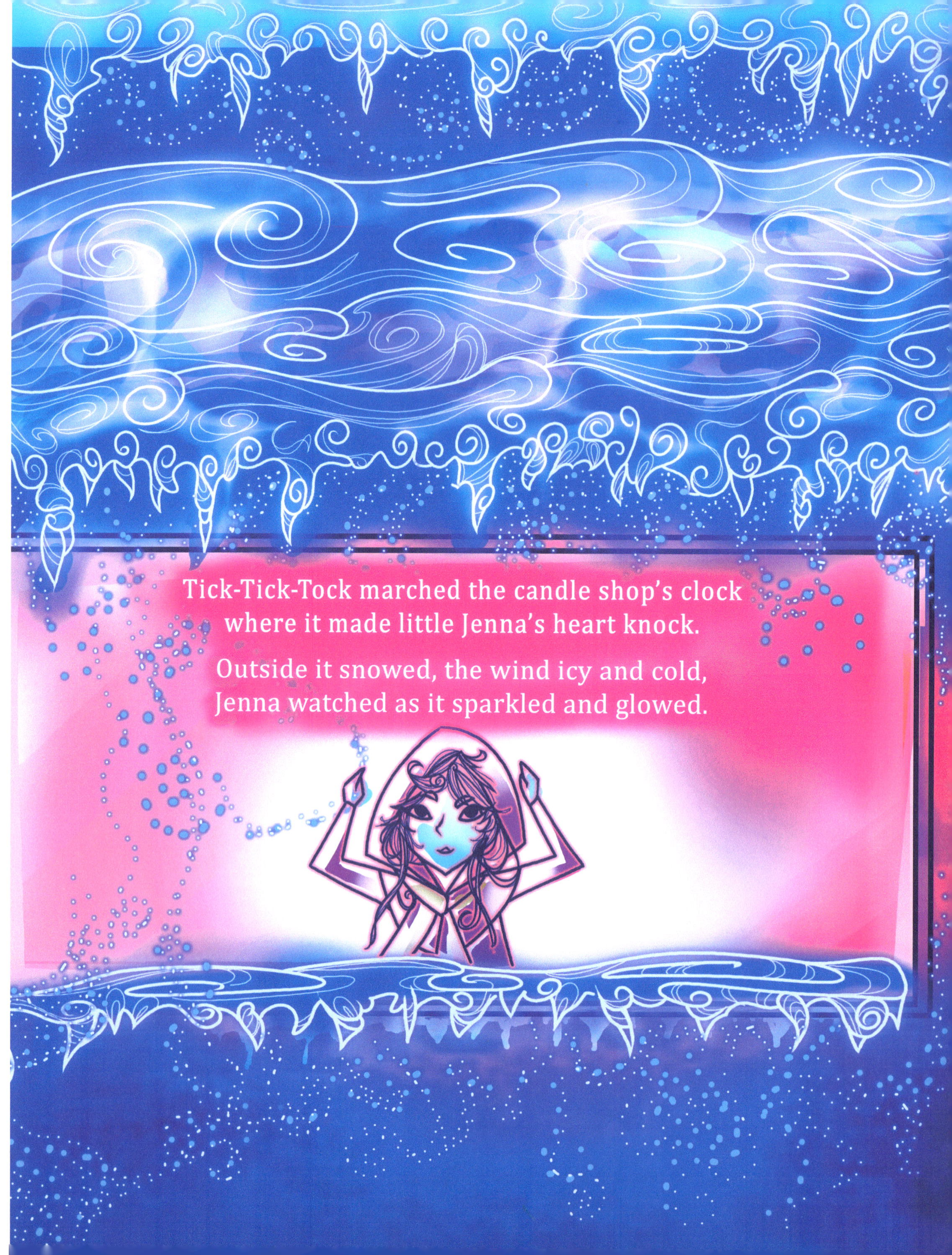

Tick-Tick-Tock marched the candle shop's clock
where it made little Jenna's heart knock.

Outside it snowed, the wind icy and cold,
Jenna watched as it sparkled and glowed.

Tick-tick GONG! chimed the clock with might,
Jenna's heart nearly plucked outright!

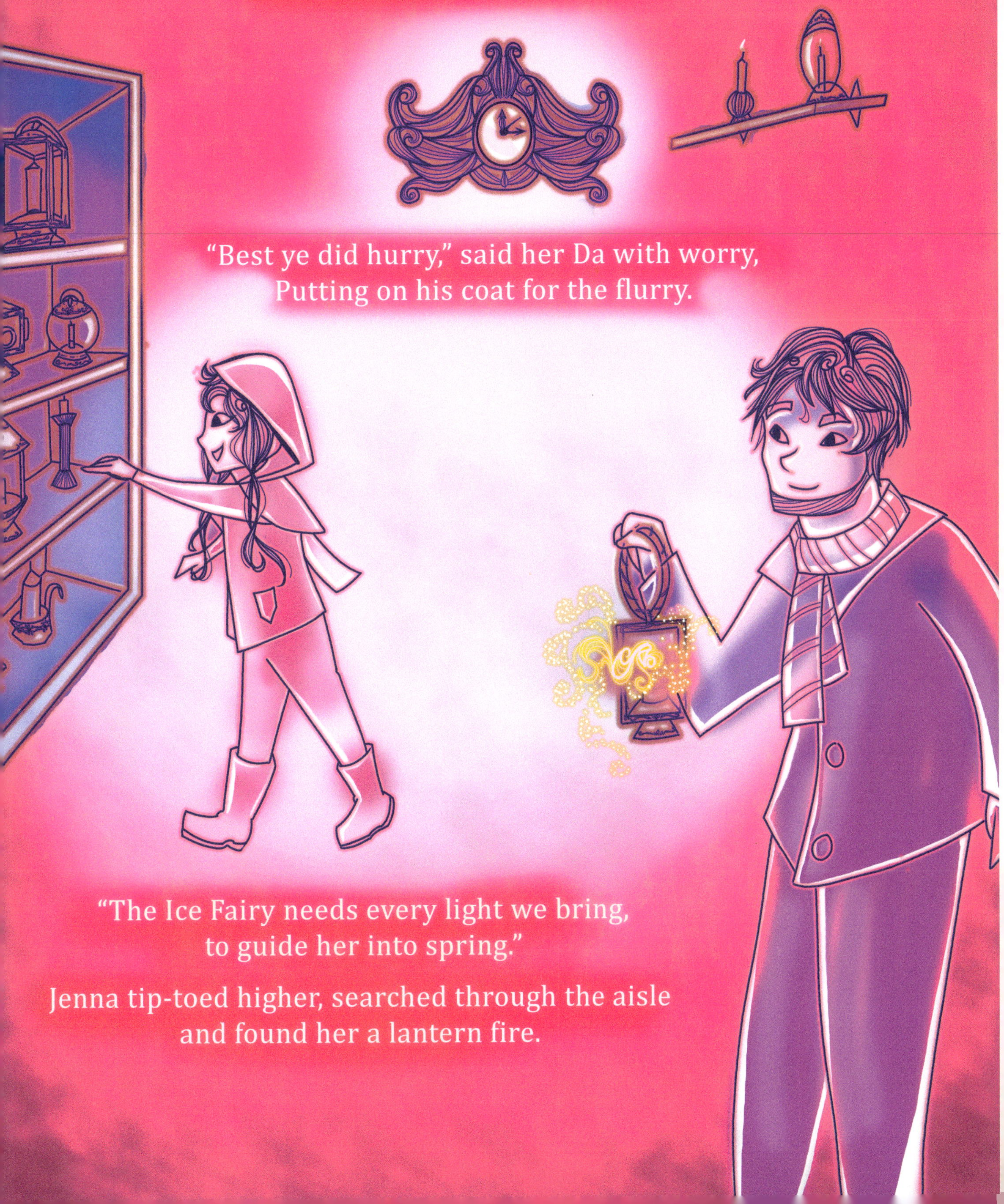

"Best ye did hurry," said her Da with worry,
Putting on his coat for the flurry.

"The Ice Fairy needs every light we bring,
to guide her into spring."

Jenna tip-toed higher, searched through the aisle
and found her a lantern fire.

"Ye know, little maid," said Jenna to the flame,
"my Ma made a song for the Fay."

"She once sang it to me, before losing her, see?
I'll sing it to ye for free."

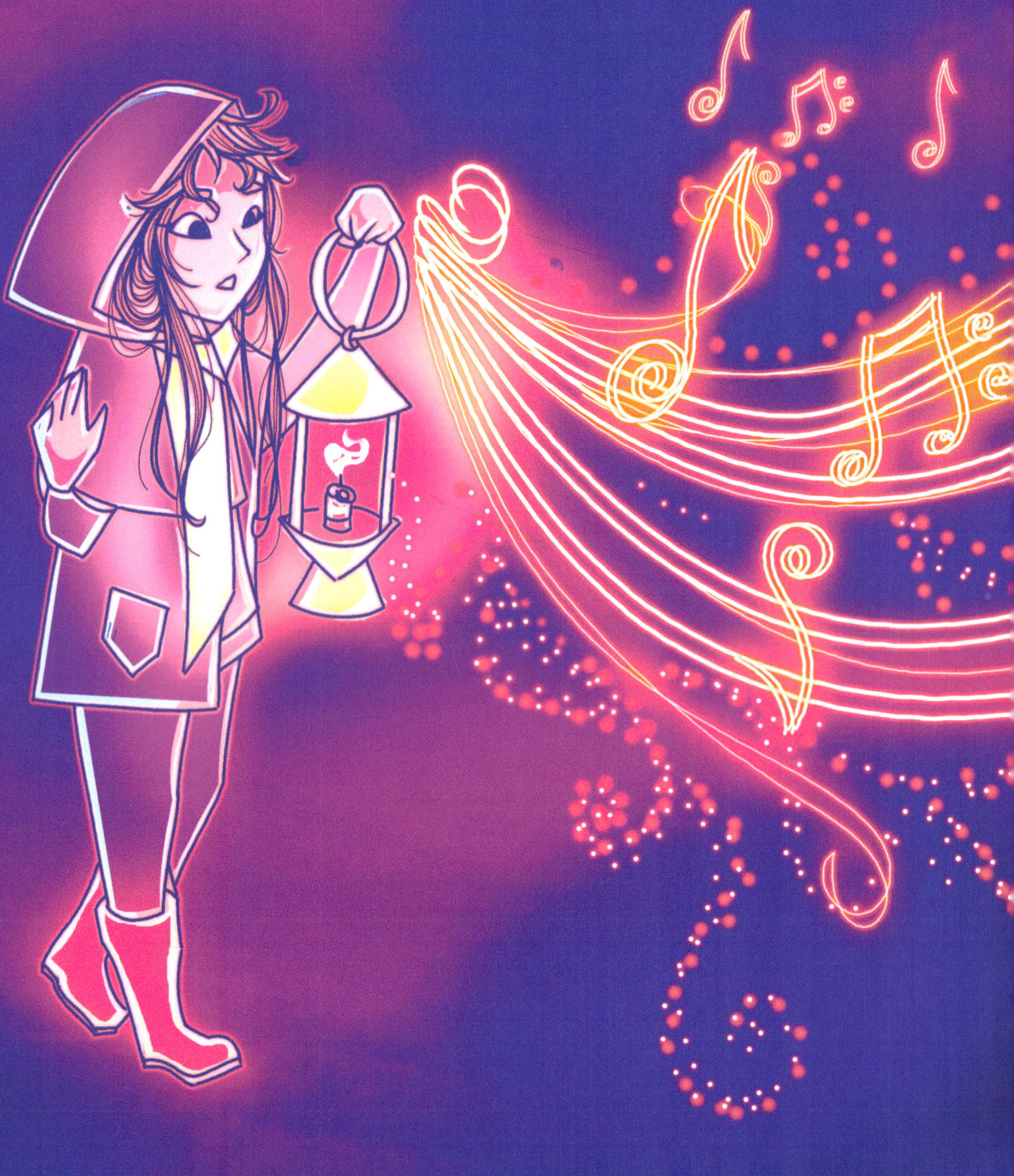

"Little light, little light, your dress so bright,
Bringing our sleep delight."

“You help our sight so we never a’fright,
as you guide our dreams in the night.”

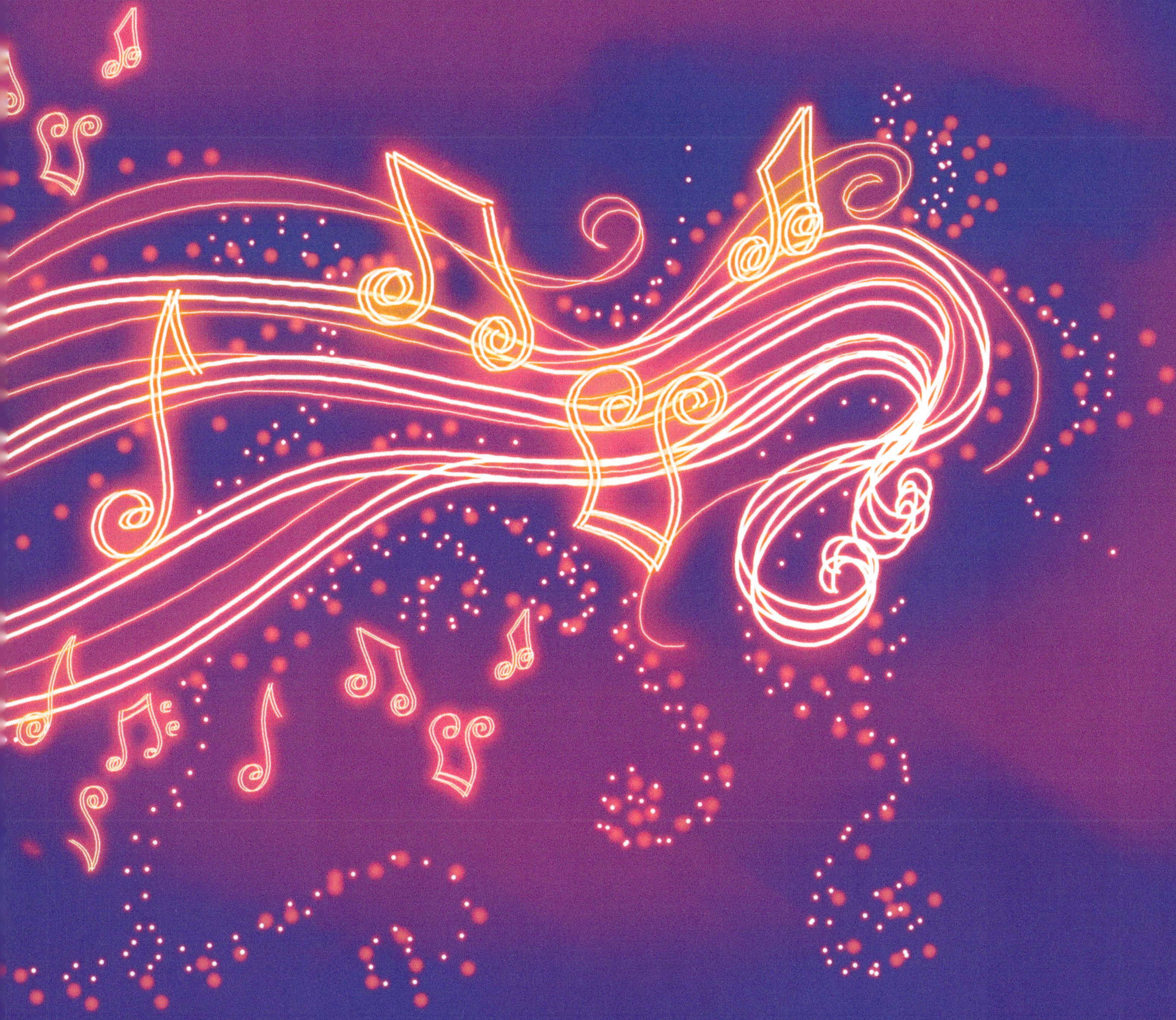

The last note hung,
Jenna's heart squeezed glum,
Her life cold without Ma's warm hug.

She shed a small tear from the pain and the fear,
The drop splashing her fire so dear.

Then her flame shined brighter,
Like a rattling pyre,
As a magical thing transpired.

It became a wee girl,
Dancing there in a twirl,
Flaming hair bouncing round with hot curls.

“My name is Adeen!” sang the fay with a gleam,
“What sad little tune did ring?”

“The first festival here, without someone quite dear,
Is the trickiest time of the year.”

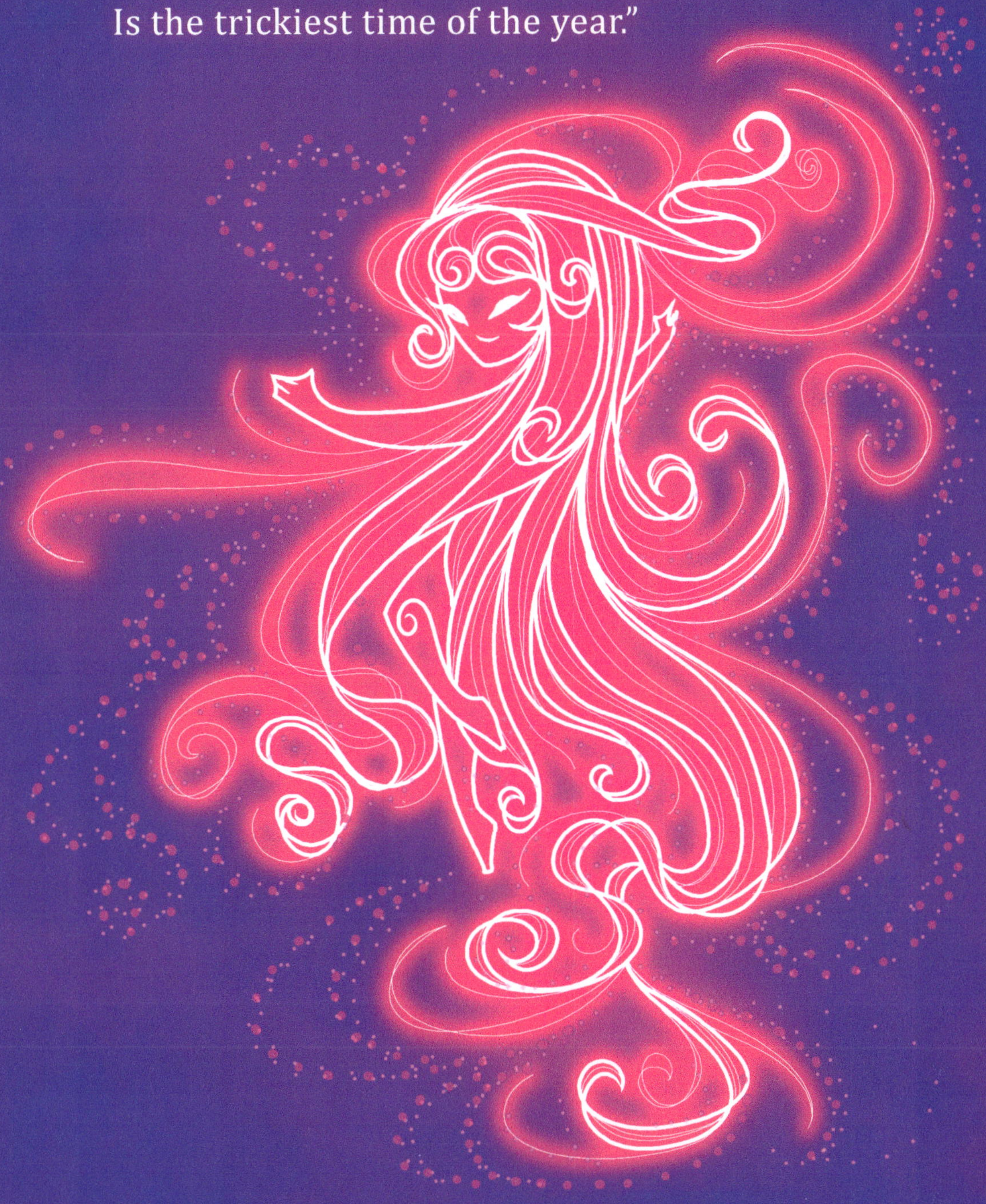

“I will keep you warm for tonight, little one,
Until spring wakes up for the morn.”

Jenna's father appeared,
Walking up near,
And Adeen hid herself like a deer.

"Da!" Jenna piped, "look, look! It's a sprite!"
But all her Da saw was a light.

They went to the pyres, the town's lanterns admired,
Snow speckled with glows from the fires.

They gathered in threes, round the great holly tree,
Save Jenna's father and she.

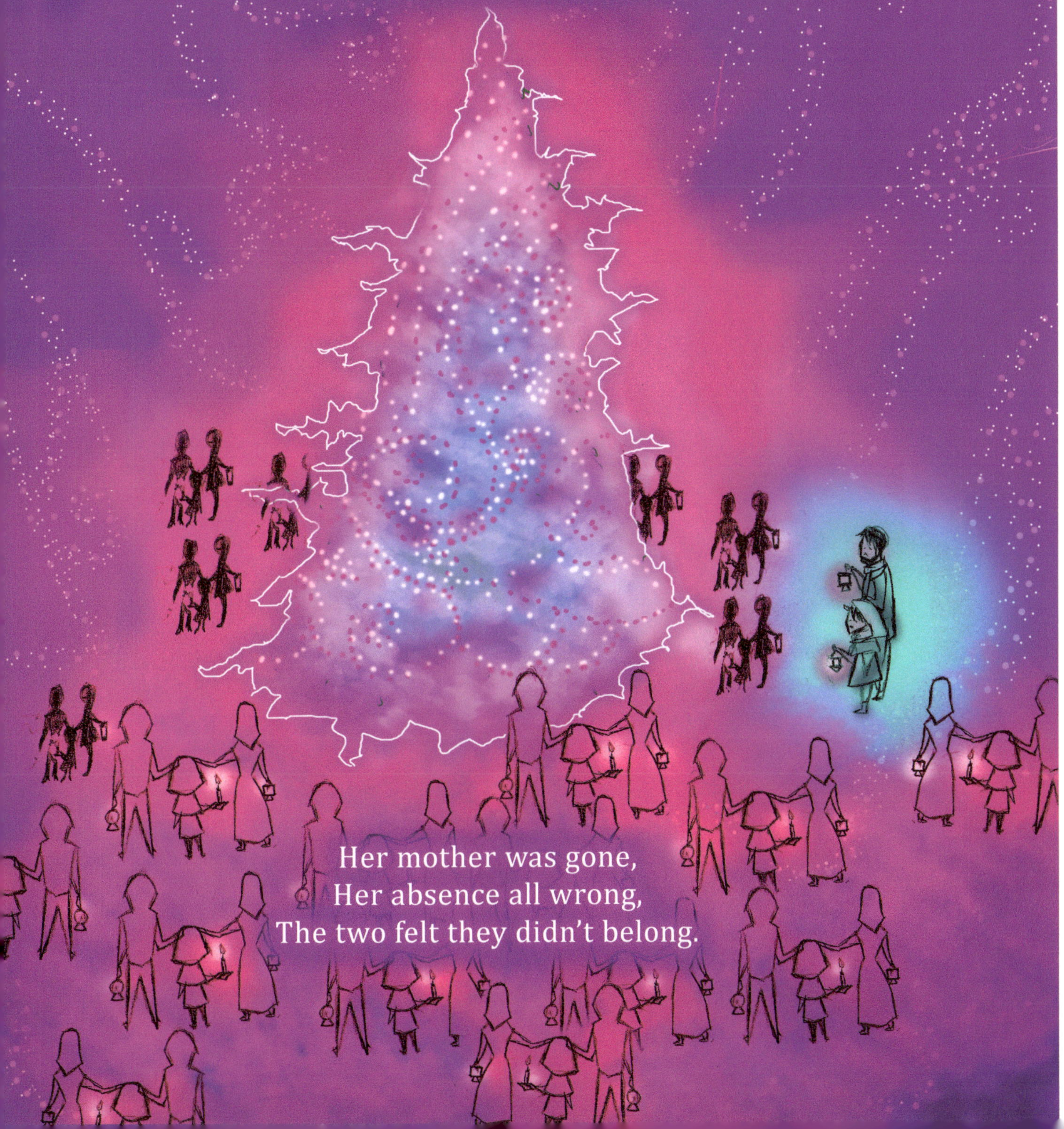

Her mother was gone,
Her absence all wrong,
The two felt they didn't belong.

But here with Adeen, as she started to sing,
Jenna heard Ma's familiar ring.

Could it be, thought she, that her little Adeen
Was Ma's soul that the fairies did bring?

But then a small chill blew over the hills,
Growing strong as it sped through the mills.

In its path came a freeze, so cold and so mean,
That it smothered the great holly tree.

All the lights were snuffed from the wind's great huff,
Save the one Jenna guarded so tough.

The village was dark, the cold leaving its mark,
And the prospect of spring grew stark.

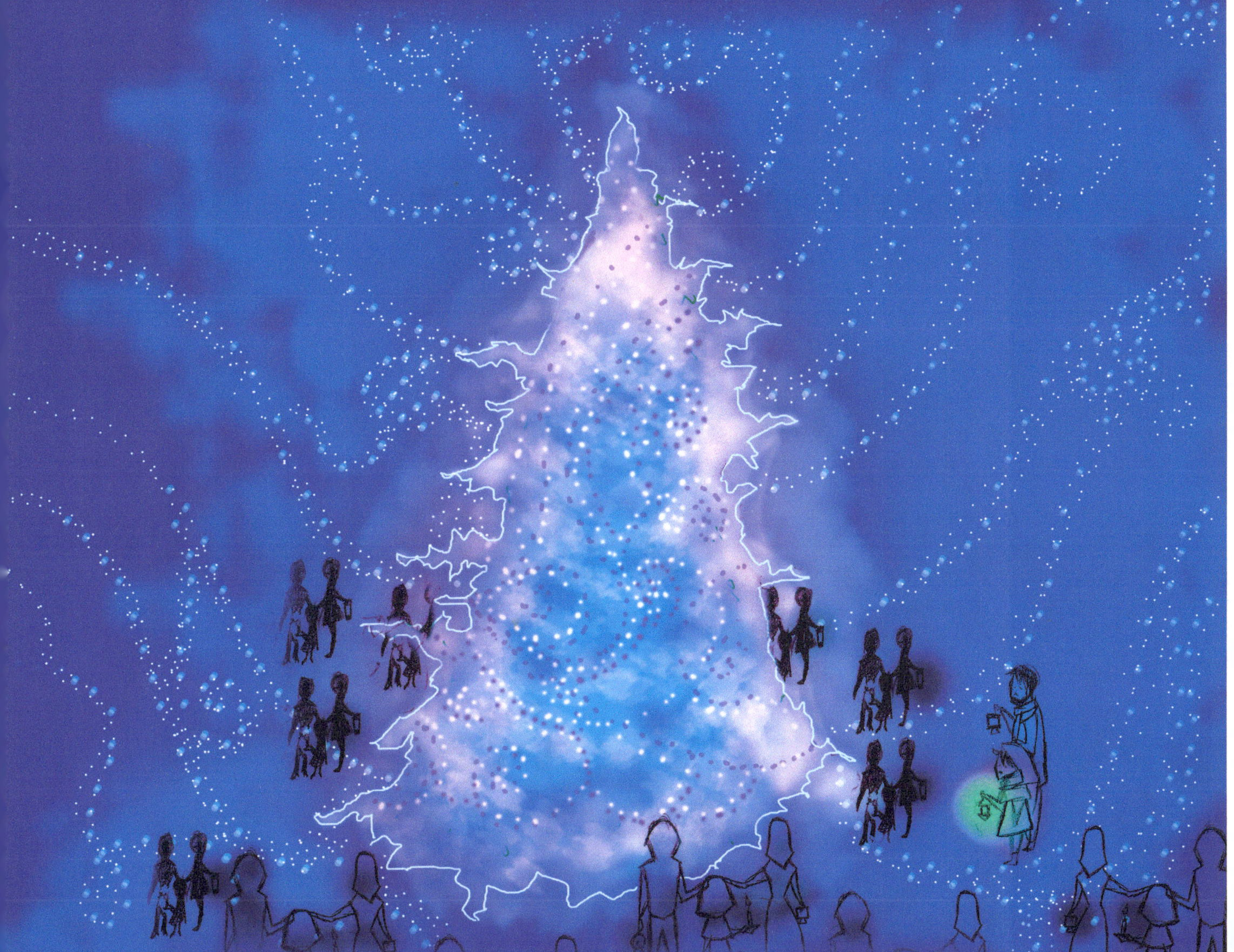

The blizzard now blasted, and oh, how it lasted!
The snow now plenty and massive.

"What will we do?" Jenna's father cried blue,
"Now the Ice Fairy's lost her view!"

Jenna held her dear light, Adeen's glow still bright,
And she made her decision outright.

"I'll find her!" said she, dashing into the freeze,
Da's shouts now faded and weak.

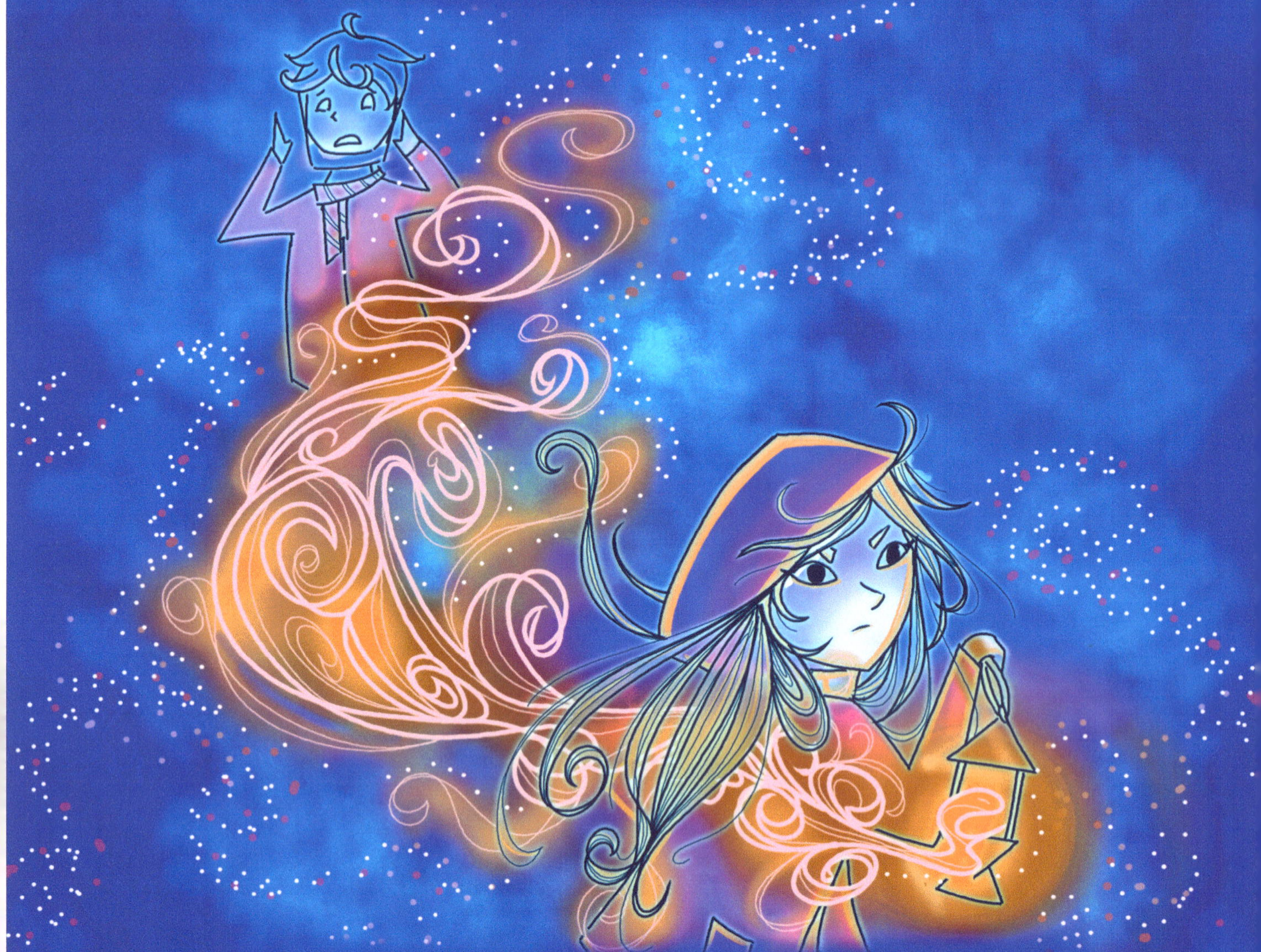

Jenna knew of the risk, the chill bitter and brisk,
But she wouldn't let Ma's soul be missed.

With winter a blunder, she'd be torn asunder,
And she'd break if she saw Adeen suffer.

With her lantern she trudged, Adeen lighting the slush,
As she guilded her through the white mush.

The flame seemed to know just where to go,
As Adeen lead her back to her home.

Under the door of her candle shop's floor,
Was a little girl, snowy and pure.

Her skin made of ice, hair glassy and nice,
She shivered and wailed with a vice!

Jenna knew it was she, the Ice Fairy indeed,
And knew exactly what she did need.

Jenna knelt with one knee and said, "Come with me!"
As she displayed her little Adeen.

The ice girl wiped tears, Adeen snuffing her fears,
To the holly tree Jenna did steer.

The wind whipped and it flipped, but steadfast Jenna kept
Adeen shielded and guarded forthwith.

The fairy followed them fast, to the holly tree's patch,
And summoned her ancient staff.

While under the branches, she breathed slow in batches,
Then swung down her staff like a hatchet.

The wind hung in the air, disappearing right there,
As the snow melted all the despair.

The sun now shone, spring flowers had grown,
As winter had finally flown.

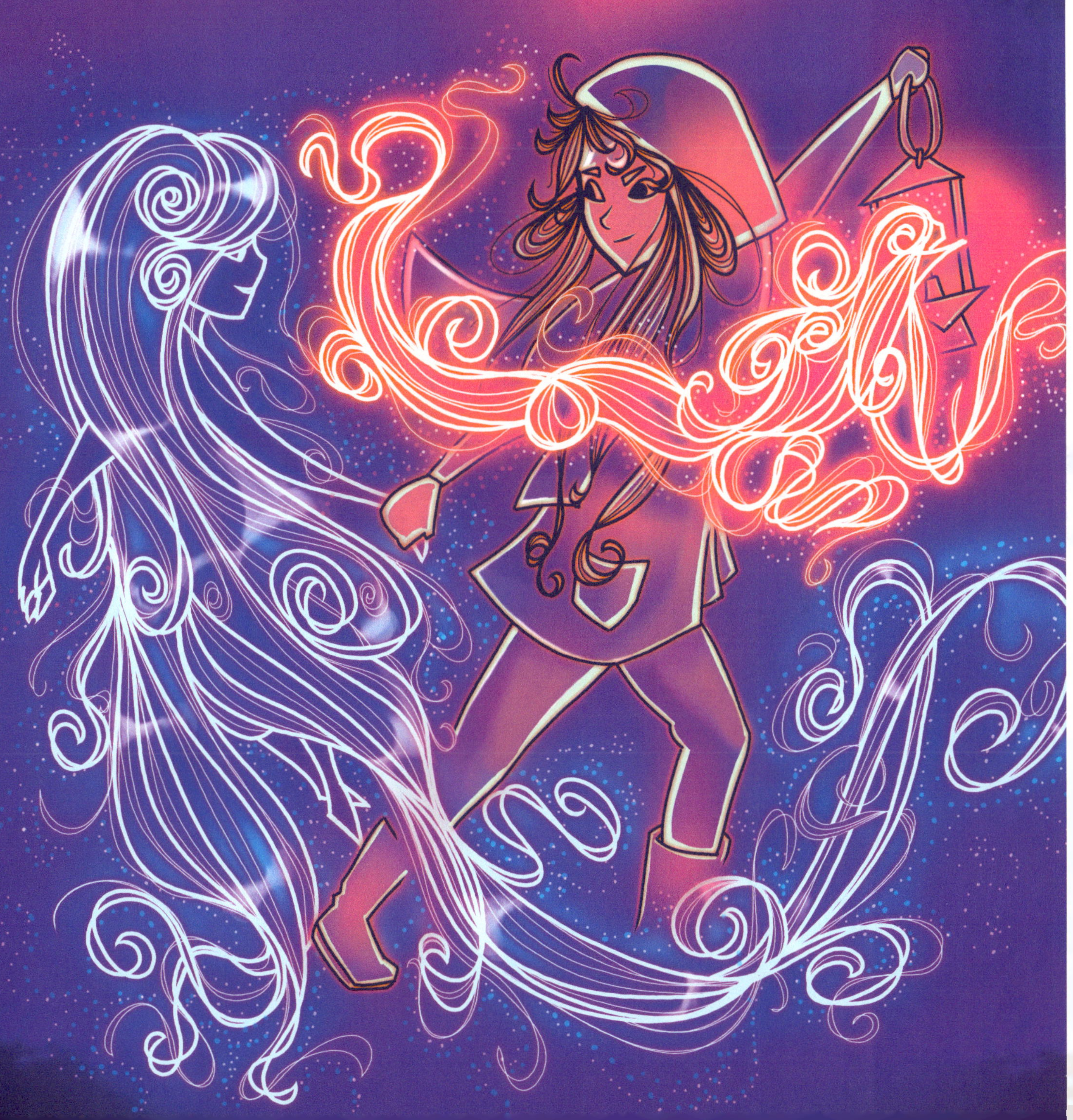

The fairy thanked Jenna along with the flame,
Then her ice changed to solid bright gold.

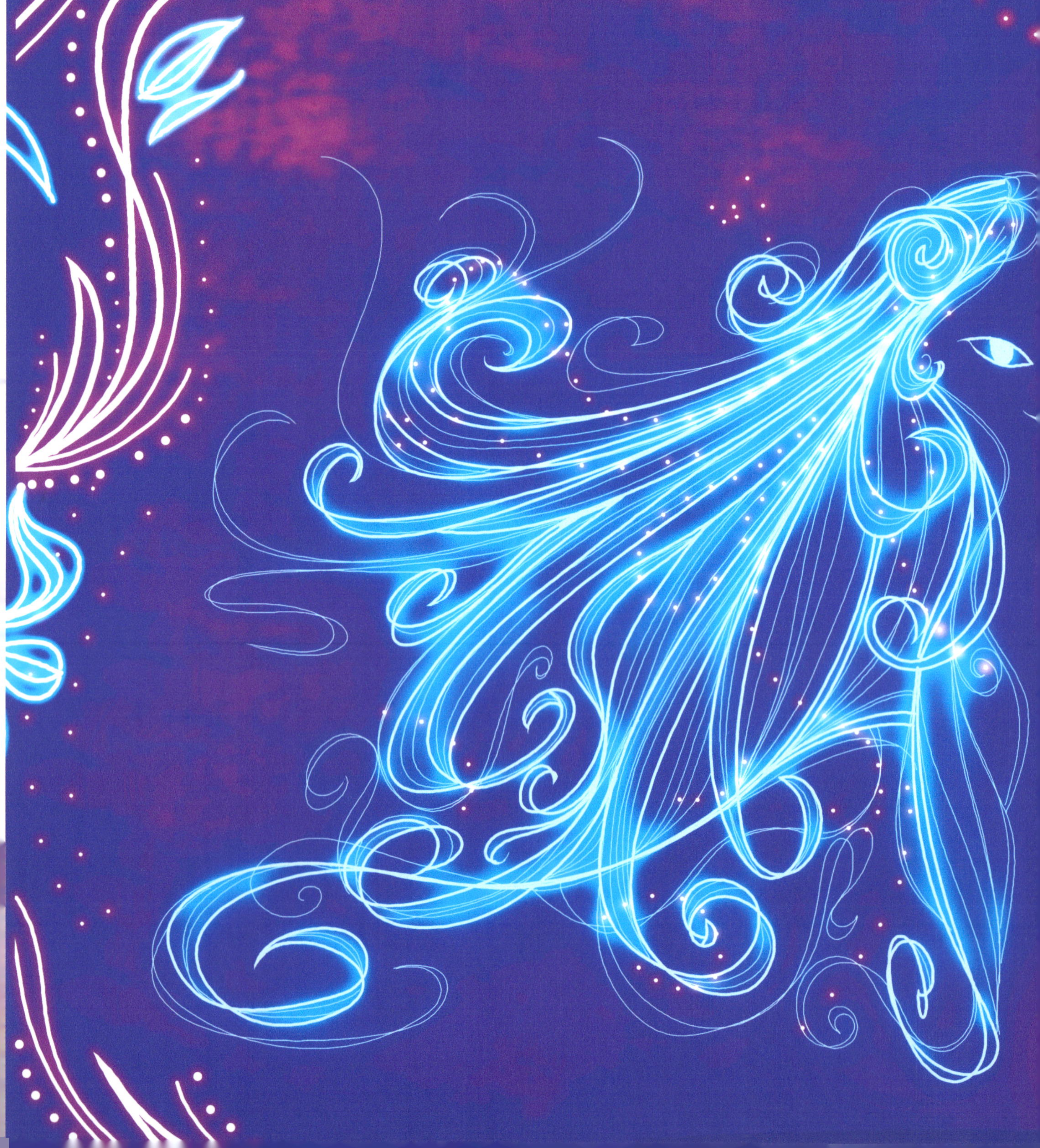

The gold fairy will stay, till autumn's first day,
When she comes for the harvest to play.

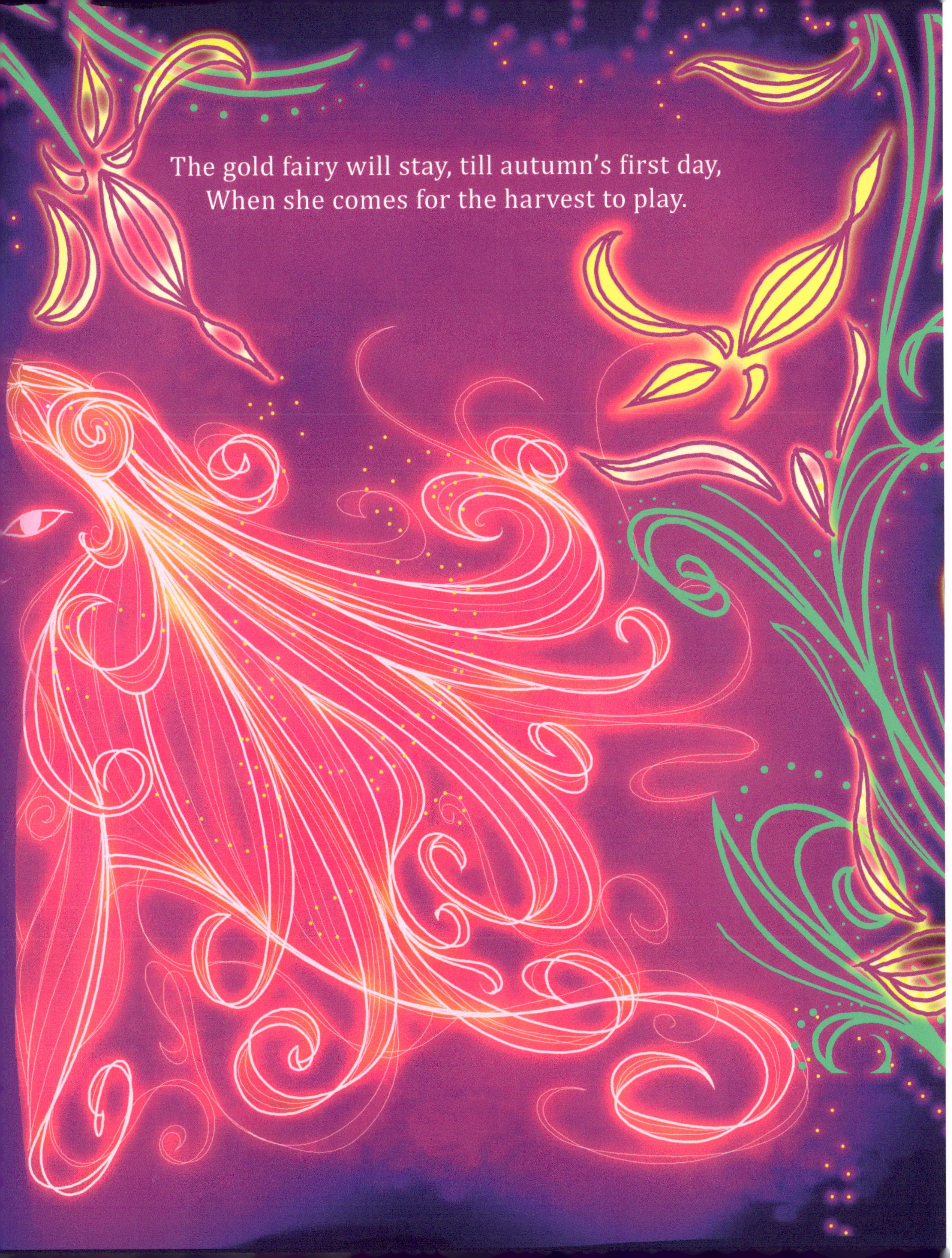

And Adeen, the wee fire, she would stay for a while,
Jenna smiled as her light didn't tire.

"Now we won't be apart," Adeen said, rather smart,
"I'm the fire that burns in your heart."

"When you're lost without cheer,
All alone, my dear,
Remember your fire will steer."

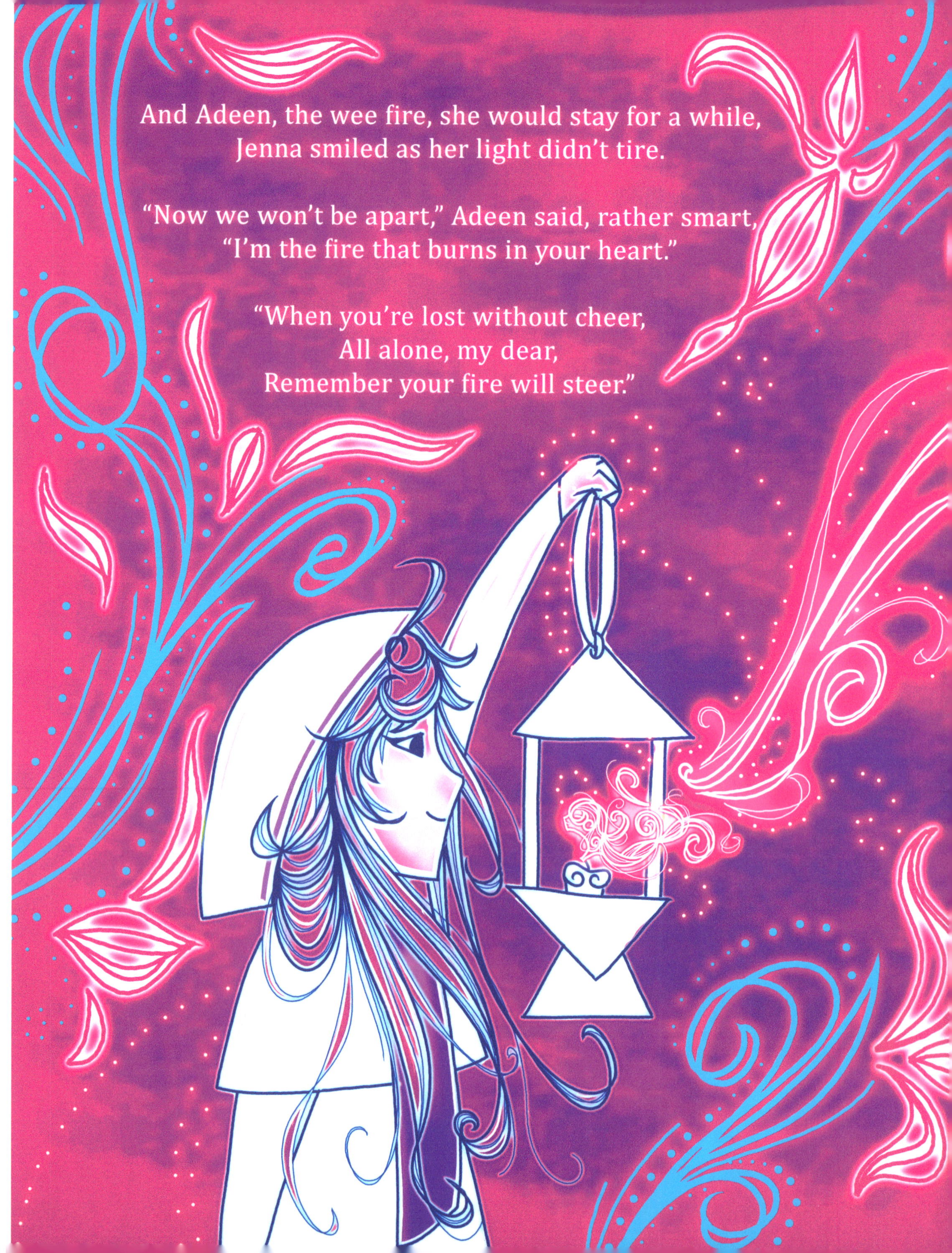

Little light, Little light, your dress so bright,
Bringing our sleep delight.

You help our sight so we never a'fright,
Guiding our dreams in the night.

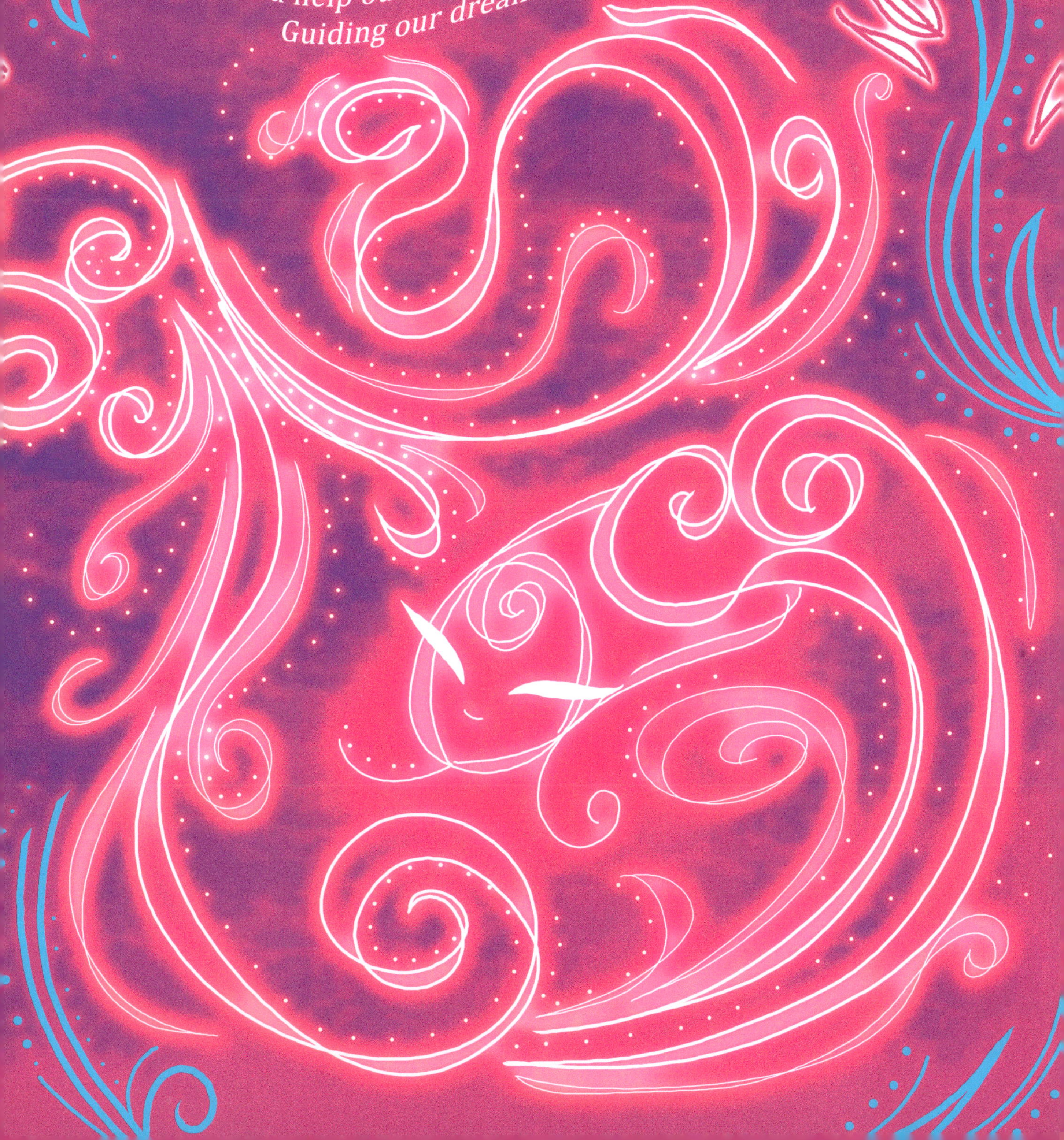

Ellie Raine is an award-winning fantasy author, the mother of a fearsome dragon princess, and a dreamer of all things whimsical.

For other works by
Ellie Raine, visit www.EllieRaine.com.

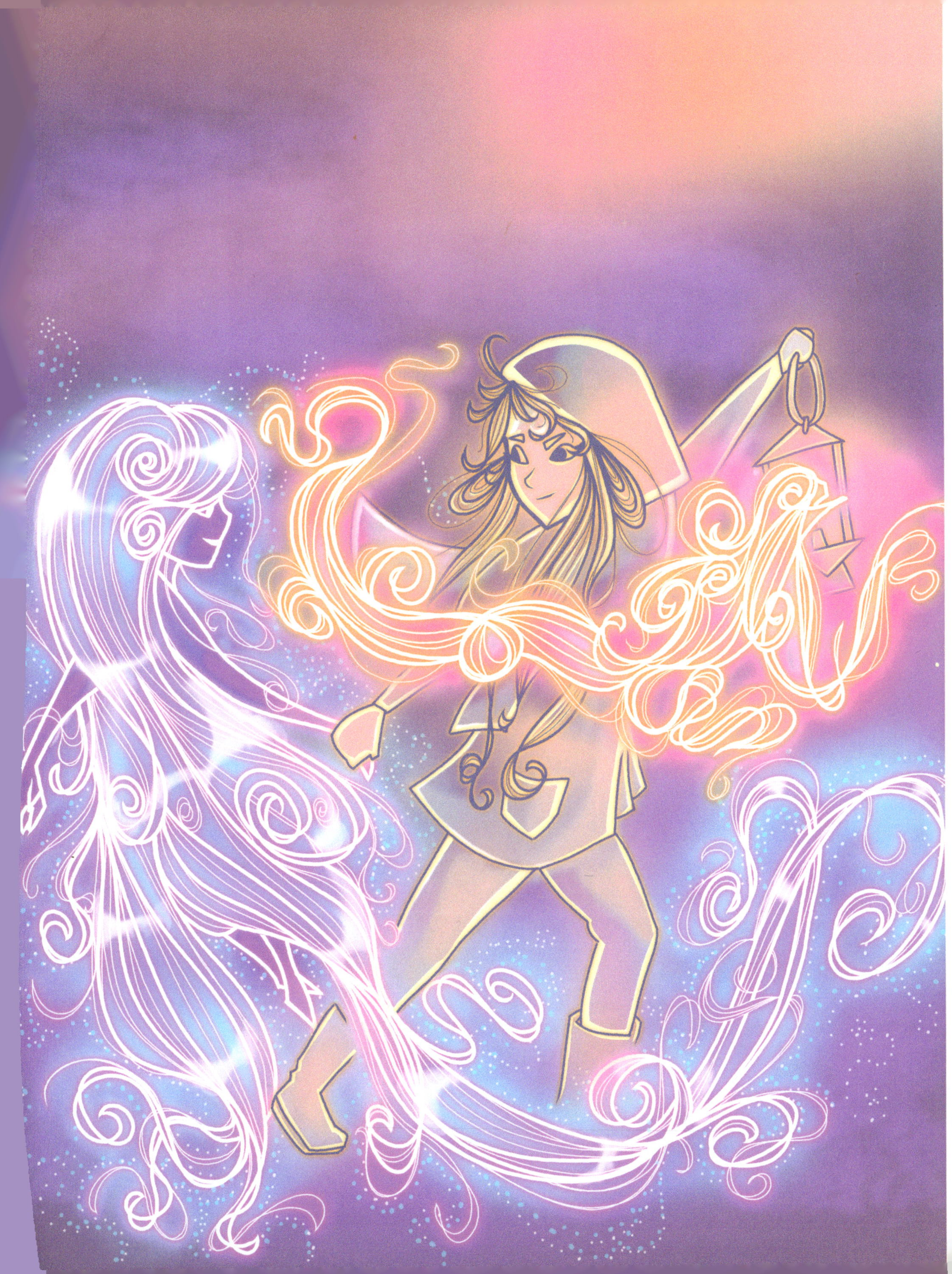

CPSIA information can be obtained
at www.ICGtesting.com
Printed in the USA
BVHW020829161120
593414BV00004B/17